WHERE'S OUR MAMA?

● ● ●

DIANE GOODE

DUTTON CHILDREN'S BOOKS   NEW YORK

for my mama

with grateful acknowledgment
to Lucia Monfried

Copyright © 1991 by Diane Goode
Library of Congress Cataloging-in-Publication Data
Goode, Diane.
Where's our mama?/ Diane Goode.
p.   cm.
Summary: A kindly gendarme conducts two young children around
Paris in search of their lost mother.
ISBN 0-525-44770-9
[1. Paris (France)—Fiction.   2. Mothers—Fiction.]   I. Title.
PZ7.G604Wh   1991
[E]—dc20   91-2158   CIP   AC

Published in the United States by Dutton Children's Books,
a division of Penguin Books USA Inc.
Designer: Riki Levinson
Printed in Hong Kong by South China Printing Co.
First Edition   10 9 8 7 6 5 4 3 2 1

When we arrived in the station, a big gust of wind blew mama's hat right off her head. "Oh, la la!" she cried. "Stay right here while I find it."

Mama ran after her hat
while we sat and waited,

and waited.

When mama still did not return, we began
to cry.

A gendarme nearby heard us.

"We have lost our mother," we sobbed.

"What is her name?" he asked.

"Mama."

"What does your mama look like?"

"Our mama is the most beautiful woman
in the world!"

"Dry your eyes, children, and we will
find her."

and waited.

When mama still did not return, we began
to cry.

A gendarme nearby heard us.

"We have lost our mother," we sobbed.

"What is her name?" he asked.

"Mama."

"What does your mama look like?"

"Our mama is the most beautiful woman
in the world!"

"Dry your eyes, children, and we will
find her."

"Is this your mama?"

"Oh, no, sir. Our mama doesn't read the newspaper. Mama reads books—millions of books."

"Is this your mama?" asked the gendarme.
"Oh, no, sir. Our mama is very strong.
Mama can carry her own parcels."

"Is this your mama?"

"Oh, no, sir. Our mama never whispers. Everyone loves mama's voice—she is famous for it."

"Is that your mama?"

"Oh, no, sir. Our mama is very slim. But
Mama cooks the best food in the world."

"Is this your mama?"

"Oh, no, sir. Our mama wears only pretty hats."

"Is that your mama?"

"Oh, no, sir. Our mama is not afraid of a mouse. Mama is very brave."

"Is that your mama?"
"Oh, no, sir. Our mama would never do that. She is very smart."

"Is that your mama?"

"Oh, no, sir. People listen when our mama speaks. Oh! I just remembered what mama said."

"Mama said we were to wait at the station."

"Is this your mama?"

"Yes, this is our mama!"